All children have
a great ambition to read
to themselves...

and a sense of achievement when they can do
so. The **read it yourself** *series has been devised*
to satisfy their ambition. Since many children
learn from the Ladybird Key Words Reading
Scheme, these stories have been based to a
large extent on the Key Words List, and the tales
chosen are those with which children are likely
to be familiar.

The series can of course be used as
supplementary reading for any reading scheme.
Dick Whittington *is intended for children reading*
up to Book 3c of the Ladybird Reading Scheme.
The following words are additional to the
vocabulary used at that level –

Dick, or, money, London, work,
walks, houses, sleep, outside, rich,
rats, cat, chases, away, far, lands,
send, runs, bells, back, be, Mayor, of,
king, captain, lends, married, soon,
Whittington *(in title only)*

A list of other titles at the same level will be
found on the back cover.

Published by Ladybird Books Ltd Loughborough Leicestershire UK
Ladybird Books Inc Lewiston Maine 04240 USA

© LADYBIRD BOOKS LTD MCMLXXVIII

Dick Whittington

by Fran Hunia
illustrated by Kathie Layfield

Ladybird Books

This is Dick.

He has no Mummy
or Daddy.

He has no money.

Dick says,

I want to go to London.

I can work in London

and get some money.

TO LONDON 150 MILES

Dick walks and walks.

A man comes.

He says, Jump up here.
You can come to London
with me.

Dick is in London.

He sees boys and girls,
shops and houses.

Dick wants to sleep.

He has no home in London.

I have to sleep here,
outside this house,
he says.

13

It is a rich man's house.

The rich man comes home.

He wants to help Dick.

You can work for me,
he says.

Dick is pleased.

The rich man has one girl.

Dick likes the girl.

Dick works and works.

He gets into bed
to sleep.

Some rats jump down
and play on the bed.

I have to get a cat,
says Dick.

Dick gets a cat.

It is a good cat.

It chases the rats away.

Dick is pleased

that he can sleep.

The rich man
has some boats
that go to far lands.

He says to Dick,
Send the cat away
on the boat,
and you can get
some money.

No, says Dick.

I like this cat.

It chases rats.

Please send the cat,
says the girl.

Dick wants to please
the girl.

He sends the cat
away on the boat.

Dick has no cat
to chase the rats away.

They jump and play
on the bed.

Dick gets up

and runs away.

The bells say to Dick,

Go back, Dick, go back.

You can be

Mayor of London.

Dick walks back

to the rich man's house.

Dick's cat works
on the boat.

It chases rats.

The boat comes to a land
far away.

The king says
to the captain of the boat,
Come home with me.

They go to the king's house.

Rats jump and play
in the king's house.

The captain says,

Have you a cat?

No, says the king.

No one in this land

has a cat.

Can a cat help me?

Can a cat chase rats away?

Yes, says the captain.

A cat can help you.

I have one on the boat.

I can get it for you.

Good, says the king.

Please get the cat for me.

The captain lends the cat
to the king.

The cat chases the rats away,
and the king is pleased.

He gives the captain
some money for Dick.

The captain is in London.

He gives the money
to Dick.

This is for you, he says.
You are a rich man, Dick.

Yes, says Dick.
The cat helped me
to get rich.

Yes, it was the cat
that helped Dick
to get rich.

Dick married
the rich man's girl,
and soon he was
Mayor of London.